GW01605765

The Romance of the Swag

The Romance of the Swag

by

HENRY LAWSON

Illustrated with WOODCUTS by LIONEL LINDSAY

Lansdowne
Sydney Auckland London New York

(1) Immigrant in Belltopper
(2) Knapsack
(3) Horse Collar
(4) Back View of Australian Swaggie.

Note: The four small woodcuts, set as headings to the stories, illustrate the evolution of the Swag, as defined by Lawson in "The Romance of the Swag" (p. 10).

Printed in Australia by Dominion Press/Hedges and Bell, Melbourne
Original hardbound edition of *The Romance of the Swag* published in Australia 1939 by the Australian Limited Editions Society in a three hundred and fifty copy edition.
Some relevant poems have been included in this edition for added interest.

Published by Lansdowne
a division of R.P.L.A. Pty. Ltd.
176 South Creek Road, Dee Why West 2099
First published in Australia in this edition 1974

Designed by Dawn Daly

National Library of Australia Cataloguing-in-Publication Data

Lawson, Henry, 1867-1922.
The romance of the swag.

Previously published: Sydney: Ure Smith, 1974.
ISBN 0 7018 1881 6.

I. Lindsay, Sir Lionel, 1874-1961. II. Title.

A828'.209

Introduction

I once came across Henry Lawson in front of The Bulletin office, clasping firmly the hands of a swagman and an aboriginal. Henry held their embarrassed hands for an unconscionable time, his eye lit up by some interior ecstasy, which I have since interpreted as the poet's mystic union with his subject matter.

As I gazed entranced at this prodigy, I became conscious of its perfect congruity; for here were Lawson's creatures in the flesh, all unconscious that they were symbols of the Bush and the Never-Never, and already immortalised in imperishable prose by the tall man with the bright, soft eyes.

It was the coincidence of the Short Story Era with the advent of the Sydney Bulletin that gave Lawson his writing chance. Maupassant and Bret Harte had established the form, and Kipling's genius was already acclaimed. J. F. Archibald, with his keen scent for any expression of the life-interest, was quick to discern the value of Lawson, Paterson, Becke and Edward Dyson, whose plain tales and character sketches became the leading literary feature of his paper. Under Archibald's critical eye, and his insistence upon precision and brevity, Lawson's work, remarkable already for its close observation of life, took definite shape and colour. It is Lawson's humanity, his humour, his knowledge of the heart, that won for him a world-wide audience. But the power to condense and dramatise, the sure instinct for the right tone and atmosphere, and above everything, the easy control of a simple vocabulary from which he could evoke any shade of expression, made him the fine prose artist with a unique place in our literature. His prose is at times careless, but it possesses a natural rhythm, and embodies all that is laconic and casual in the Australian character.

The stories in this volume were selected for their swagman interest with a view to consistent illustration. "The Romance of the Swag" was written in England and Lawson gave it a didactic turn that there might be no confusion of the Australian Swagman with the Common Tramp: and it is well that he gave us this lore of the swag – a precious piece of Australian folk-lore – now that the last Sundowner has disappeared into the dust of the Sunset Track.

My own interest in this high matter goes back to my childhood in Creswick. Our home faced a wide common, and with the seasonal accumulation of blue metal on the corner an old swaggie returned, like some homing bird, to engage upon the delicate business of splitting the stones. My hands itched to use those perfect hammers with their steel-grey heads and white wattle handles: but the old breaker, cunning as Tom Sawyer, and growling the while about the scarcity of good wattle-sticks, was always long in giving me an ungracious permission to swell the heap. He was a taciturn old man like most of his kind, yet he pitched such a piteous tale about his broken boots, "cut by the cruel stones," that my heart was rent with compassion and I gave him my father's second-best pair of boots. There was a long search afterwards for those boots; but as I was never directly questioned the mystery has had to wait upon this occasion for its solution.

Later on I came to illustrate the swaggie jokes for The Bulletin, and as I wished to collect as many "variants" as possible, I was always on the look-out for any stray Murrumbidgee whaler, short of half-a-crown, to pose for me: the types I have used in the woodcuts are therefore contemporaries of Lawson's characters.

Lawson never wrote anything better than "Rats" and "Enter Mitchell." In the compass of a page or two and without the least sense of compression, he achieves the perfect artistic unity. The prose is fine as the portraiture , as for the humour, it is Lawson's alone. The "Two Sundowners" are slightly generalised, representatives of that vanished race – gone with the fairies – who were content to spend existence tramping from station to station, to collect before sundown the sacrosanct ration of a "pannikin of dust" and a pinch of tea and sugar. They belong to that ancient community of rascals which engaged the interest of Chaucer and Shakespeare, Burns and Mark Twain, Rabelais and Villon, Cervantes, Quevedo, and the unknown author of Lazarillo de Tormes, and are by no means the least of their company. The type is eternal and will last so long as there exist laws to be dodged and honest work evaded. If I may speak for myself, I must say that I am more grateful to Lawson for such humours than for all his powers of pathos. "Man was made to mourn," but he invented humour, which is the salt of life, and, as I like to think, the rarest of his many inventions.

Lawson was as much a sour moralist as Burns. He accepted life on its face value, and that he extended as wide a sympathy to his two hopeless old wasters, as to the stark tragedy of the "Drover's Wife," is the hallmark of his greatness.

Lionel Lindsay
1939

Contents

Short Stories

Poems

The Romance of the Swag

THE AUSTRALIAN SWAG FASHION IS THE EASIEST way in the world of carrying a load. I ought to know something about carrying loads: I've carried babies, which are the heaviest and most awkward and heart-breaking loads in this world for a boy or man to carry, I fancy. God remember mothers who slave about the housework (and do sometimes a man's work in addition in the Bush) with a heavy, squalling kid on one arm! I've humped logs on the Selection, "burning-off," with loads of fencing posts and rails and palings out of steep, rugged gullies (and was happier then, perhaps); I've carried a shovel, crowbar, heavy "rammer," a dozen insulators on an average (strung round my shoulders with raw flax) – to say nothing of soldering kit, tucker bag, billy and climbing spurs – all day on a telegraph line in rough country in New Zealand, and in places where a man had to manage his load with one hand and help himself climb with the other; and I've helped hump and drag telegraph poles up cliffs and sidings where the horses couldn't go. I've carried a portmanteau on the hot dusty roads in green old Jackeroo days. Ask any actor who's been stranded and had to count railway sleepers from one town to another! he'll tell you what sort of an awkward load a portmanteau is, especially if there's a broken-hearted man underneath it. I've tried knapsack fashion – one of the least healthy and most likely to give a man sores; I've carried my belongings in a three-bushel sack slung over my shoulder – blankets, tucker, spare boots and poetry all lumped together. I tried carrying a load on my head, and got a crick in my neck and spine for days. I've carried a load on my mind that should have been shared by editors and publishers. I've helped hump luggage and furniture up to, and down from, a top flat in London. And I've carried swag for months out-back in Australia – and it was life, in spite of its "squalidness" and meanness and wretchedness and hardship, and in spite of the fact that the world would have regarded us as "tramps" – and a free life amongst *men* from all the world!

The Australian swag was born of Australia and no other land – of the Great Lone Land of magnificent distances and bright heat; the land of Self-reliance, and Never-give-in, and Help-your-mate.

The grave of many of the world's tragedies and comedies – royal and otherwise. The land where a man out of employment might shoulder his swag in Adelaide and take the track, and years later walk into a hut on the Gulf, or never be heard of any more, or a body be found in the Bush and buried by the mounted police, or never found and never buried – what does it matter?

The land I love above all others – not because it was kind to me, but because I was born on Australian soil, and because of the foreign father who died at his work in the ranks of Australian pioneers, and because of many things. Australia! my country! her very name is music to me. God bless Australia! for the sake of the great hearts of the heart of her! God keep her clear of the old-world shams and social lies and mockery, and callous commercialism, and sordid shame! and Heaven send that, if ever in my time her sons are called upon to fight for her young life and honour, I die with the first rank of them and be buried in Australian ground.

But this will probably be called false, forced or "maudlin sentiment" here in England, where the mawkish sentiment of the music halls, and the popular applause it receives, is enough to make a healthy man sick, and is only equalled by music-hall vulgarity. So I'll get on.

In the old digging days the knapsack, or straps-across-the-chest fashion, was tried, but the load pressed on a man's chest and impeded his breathing, and a man needs to have his bellows free on long tracks in hot, stirless weather. Then the "horse-collar," or rolled military overcoat style – swag over one shoulder and under the other arm – was tried, but it was found to be too hot for the Australian climate, and was discarded along with Wellington boots and leggings. Until recently, Australian city artists and editors – who knew as much about the Bush as Downing Street knows about the British colonies in general – seemed to think the horse-collar swag was still in existence; and some artists gave the swagman a stick, as if he were a tramp of civilisation with an eye on the backyard and a fear of the dog. English artists, by the way, seem firmly convinced that the Australian bushman is born in Wellington boots with a polish on 'em you could shave yourself by.

The swag is usually composed of a tent "fly" or strip of calico (a cover for the swag and a shelter in bad weather – in New Zealand it is oilcloth or waterproof twill), a couple of blankets, blue by custom and preference, as that colour shows the dirt less than any other (hence the name "bluey" for swag), and the core is composed of spare clothing and small personal effects. To make or "roll up" your swag: lay the fly or strip of calico on the ground, blueys on top of it; across one end, with eighteen inches or so to spare, lay your spare trousers, shirt, etc., folded, light boots tied together by the laces toe to heel, books, bundle of old letters, portraits, or whatever little knick-knacks you have or care to carry, bag of needles, thread, pen and ink, spare patches for your pants, bootlaces, etc., lay or arrange the pile so that it will roll evenly with the swag (some pack the lot in an old pillowslip or canvas bag), take a fold over of blanket and calico the whole length on each side, so as to reduce the width of the swag to, say, three feet, throw the spare end, with an inward fold, over the little pile of belongings, and then roll the whole to the other end, using your knees and judgment to make the swag tight, compact and artistic; when within eighteen inches of the loose end take an inward fold in that, and bring it up against the body of the swag. There is a strong suggestion of a roley-poley in a rag about the business, only the ends of the swag are folded in, in rings, and not tied. Fasten the swag with three or four straps, according to judgment and the supply of straps. To the top strap, for the swag is carried (and eased down in shanty bars and against walls or verandah-posts when not on the track) in a more or less vertical position – to the top strap, and lowest, or lowest but one, fasten the ends of the shoulder strap (usually a towel is preferred as being softer to the shoulder), your coat being carried outside the swag at the back, under the straps. To the top strap fasten the string of the nose-bag, a calico bag about the size of a pillowslip, containing the tea, sugar and flour bags, bread, meat, baking powder, salt, etc., and brought, when the swag is carried from the left shoulder, over the right on to the chest, and so balancing the swag behind. But a swagman can throw a heavy swag in a nearly vertical position against his spine, slung from one shoulder only and without any balance, and carry it as easily as you might wear your overcoat. Some Bushmen arrange their belongings so neatly and conveniently, with swag straps in a sort of harness, that they can roll up the swag in about a minute, and unbuckle it and throw it out as easily as a roll of wall-paper, and there's the bed ready on the ground with the wardrobe for a pillow. The swag is always used for a seat on the track; it is a soft seat, so trousers last a long time. And, the dust being mostly soft and silky on the long tracks outback, boots last marvellously. Fifteen miles a day is the average with the swag, but you must travel according to the water: if the next bore or tank is five miles on, and the next twenty beyond, you camp at the five-mile water to-night and do the twenty next day. But if it's thirty miles you have to do it. Travelling with the swag in Australia is variously and picturesquely described as "humping bluey," "walking Matilda," "humping Matilda," "humping your drum," "being on the wallaby," "jabbing trotters," and "tea and sugar burglaring," but most travelling shearers now call themselves trav'lers, and say simply "on the track," or "carrying swag."

And there you have the Australian swag. Men from all the world have carried it – lords and low-class Chinamen, saints and world martyrs, and felons, thieves and murderers, educated gentlemen and boors who couldn't sign their mark, gentlemen who fought for Poland and convicts who fought the world, women, and more than one woman disguised as a man. The Australian swag has held in its core letters and papers in all languages, the honour of great houses, and more than one national secret, papers that would send well-known and highly-respected men to jail, and proofs of the innocence of men going mad in prisons, life tragedies and comedies, fortunes and papers that secured titles and fortunes, and the last pence of lost fortunes, life secrets, portraits of mothers and dead loves, pictures of fair women, heart-breaking old letters written long ago by vanished hands, and the pencilled manuscript of more than one book which will be famous yet.

The weight of the swag varies from the light rouseabout's swag, containing one blanket and a clean shirt, to the "royal Alfred," with tent and all complete, and weighing part of a ton. Some old sundowners have a mania for gathering, from selectors' and shearers' huts, dust heaps, etc., heart-breaking loads of rubbish which can never be of any possible use to them or anyone else. Here is an inventory of the contents of the swag of an old tramp who was found dead on the track, lying on his face on the sand, with his swag on top of him, and his arms stretched straight out as if he were embracing the Mother Earth, or had made, with his last movement, the Sign of the Cross to the blazing heavens:

Rotten old tent in rags. Filthy blue blanket, patched with squares of red and calico. Half of "white blanket," nearly black now, patched with pieces of various material and sewn to half of red blanket. Three-bushel sack slit open. Pieces of sacking. Part of a woman's skirt. Two rotten old pairs of moleskin trousers. One leg of a pair of trousers. Back of a shirt. Half a waistcoat. Two tweed coats, green, old and rotting, and patched with calico, blanket, etc. Large bundle of assorted rags for patches, all rotten. Leaky billy can, containing fishing-line, papers, suet, needles and cotton, etc., etc. Jam tin, medicine bottles, corks on strings, to hang to his hat to keep the flies off (a sign of madness in the bush, for the corks would madden a sane man sooner than the flies could). Three boots of different sizes, all belonging to the right foot, and a left slipper. Coffee-pot, without handle or spout, and quart-pot full of rubbish – broken knives and forks, with the handles burnt off, spoons, etc., etc., picked up on rubbish heaps; and many rusty nails, to be used as buttons, I suppose.

Broken saw blade, hammer, broken crockery, old pannikins, small rusty frying-pan without a handle, children's old shoes, many bits of old boot leather and green hide, part of yellow-back novel, mutilated English dictionary, grammar and arithmetic book, a ready reckoner, a cookery book, a bulgy Anglo-foreign dictionary, part of a Shakespeare, book in French and book in German, and a book on etiquette and courtship. A heavy pair of blucher boots, with uppers parched and cracked, and soles so patched (patch over patch) with leather, boot protectors, hoop iron and hobnails that they were about two inches thick, and the boots weighed over five pounds. (If you don't believe me go into the Melbourne Museum, where, in a glass case in a place of honour, you will see a similar, perhaps the same, pair of bluchers labelled "An Example of Colonial Industry.") And in the core of the swag was a sugar bag tied tightly with a whip-lash, and containing another old skirt, rolled very tight and fastened with many turns of a length of clothesline, which last, I suppose, he carried to hang himself with if he felt that way. The skirt was rolled round a small packet of old portraits and almost indecipherable letters – one from a woman who had evidently been a sensible woman and a widow, and who stated in the letter that she did not intend to get married again as she had enough to do already, slavin' her finger-nails off to keep a family, without having a second husband to keep. And her answer was "final for good and all," and it wasn't no use comin' "bungfoodlin' " round her again. If he did she'd set Satan on to him. "Satan" was a dog, I suppose.

The letter was addressed to "Dear Bill," as were others. There were no envelopes. The letters were addressed from no place in particular, so there weren't any means of identifying the dead man. The police buried him under a gum, and a young trooper cut on the tree the words:

SACRED
TO THE MEMORY OF
BILL
WHO DIED

Two Sundowners

HEEP STATIONS IN AUSTRALIA ARE ANY DISTANCE from twenty to a hundred miles apart, to keep well within the boundaries of truth and the great pastoral country. Shearing at any one shed only lasts a few weeks in the year; the number of men employed is according to the size of the shed – from three to five men in the little bough-covered shed of the small "cockatoo," up to 150 or 200 hands all told in the big corrugated iron machine shed of a pastoral company.

Shearing starts early up in northern Queensland, where you can get a "January shed"; and further south, in February, March or April sheds, and so on down to New South Wales, where shearing often lasts over Christmas. Shearers travel from shed to shed; some go a travel season without getting a pen, and an unlucky shearer might ride or tramp for several seasons and never get hands in wool; and all this explains the existence of the "footman" with his swag and the horseman with his pack-horse. They have a rough life, and the Australian shearers are certainly the most democratic and perhaps the most independent, intelligent and generous body of workmen in the world.

Shearers at a shed elect their own cook, pay him so much a head, and they buy their rations in the lump from the station store; and "travellers", i.e., shearers and rouseabouts travelling for work, are invited, as a matter of course, to sit down to the shearers' table. Also a certain allowance of tea, sugar, flour and meat is still made to travellers at most Western station stores; so it would be rather surprising if there weren't some who travelled on the game. The swagman loafer, or "bummer," times himself, especially in bad weather, to arrive at the shed just about sundown; he is then sure of "tea," shelter for the night, breakfast, and some tucker from the cook to take him on along the track. Brummy and Swampy were sundowners.

Swampy was a bummer born – and proud of it. Brummy had drifted down to loaferdom, and his nature was soured and his spirit revengeful against the world because of the memory of early years wasted at hard work and in being honest. Both were short and stout, and both had scrubby beards, but Brummy's beard was a dusty black and Swampy's fiery red – he indulged in a monkey-shave sometimes, but his lower face was mostly like a patch of coarse stubble with a dying hedge round it. They had travelled together for a long time. They seemed at times to hate each other with a murderous hatred, but they were too lazy to fight. Sometimes they'd tramp side by side and growl at each other by the hour, other times they'd sulk for days; one would push on ahead and the other drop behind until there was a mile or two between them; but one always carried the billy, or the sugar, or something that was necessary to the comfort of the other, so they'd come together at sundown. They had travelled together a long time, and perhaps that was why they hated each other. They often agreed to part and take different tracks, and sometimes they parted – for a while. They agreed in cadging, and cadged in turn. They carried a spare set of tucker-bags, and if, for instance, they were out of sugar and had plenty of flour and tea, Brummy or Swampy would go to the store, boundary-rider's hut, or selector's, with the sugar bag in his hand and the other bags in his shirt front on spec. He'd get the sugar first, and then, if it looked good enough, the flour bag would come out, then the tea bag. And before he left he'd remark casually that he and his mate hadn't had a smoke for two days. They never missed a chance. And when they'd cadged more tucker than they could comfortably carry, they'd camp for a day or two and eat it down. Sometimes they'd have as much as a pound of tobacco, all in little "borrowed" bits, cut from the sticks or cakes of honest travellers. They never missed a chance. If a stranger gave Swampy his cake of tobacco with the instruction to "cut off a pipeful," Swampy would cut off as much as he thought judicious, talking to the stranger and watching his eye all the time, and hiding his palm as much as possible – and sometimes, when he knew he'd cut off more than he could cram into his pipe, he'd put his hand in his pocket for the pipe and drop some of the tobacco there. Then he'd hand the plug to his mate, engage the stranger in conversation and try to hold his eye or detract his attention from Brummy, so as to give Brummy a chance of cutting off a couple of pipefuls, and, maybe, nicking off a corner of the cake and slipping it into his pocket. I once heard a bushman say that no one but a skunk would be guilty of this tobacco trick – that it is about the meanest trick a man could be capable of – *because it spoils the chances of the next hard-up swaggy who asks the victim for tobacco.*

When Brummy and Swampy came to a shed where shearing was in full swing, they'd inquire, first thing, and with some show of anxiety, if there was any chance of gettin' on; if the shed was full-handed they'd growl about hard times, wonder what the country was coming to; talk about their missuses and kids that they'd left in Sydney, curse the squatters and the Government, and, next morning, get a supply of rations from the cook and depart with looks of gloom. If, on the other hand, there was room in the shed for one or both of them, and the boss told them to go to work in the morning, they'd keep it quiet from the cook if possible, and depart, after breakfast, unostentatiously.

Sometimes, at the beginning of a drought, when the tall dead grass was like tinder for hundreds of miles and a carelessly-dropped match would set the whole country on fire, Swampy would strike a hard-faced squatter, manager, or overseer with a cold eye, and the conversation would be somewhat as follows:

Swampy: "Good-day, boss!"

Boss (shortly): "'Day."

Swampy: "Any chance of a job?"

Boss: "Naw. Got all I want and we don't start for a fortnight."

Swampy: "Can I get a bit o' meat?"

Boss: "Naw! Don't kill till Saturday."

Swampy: "Pint o' flour?"

Boss: "Naw. Short ourselves."

Swampy: "Bit o' tea or sugar, boss?"

Boss: "Naw – what next?"

Swampy: "Bit o' baccer, boss. Ain't had a smoke for a week."

Boss: "Naw. Ain't got enough for meself till the wagon comes out."

Swampy: "Ah, well! It's hot, ain't it, boss?"

Boss: "Yes – it's hot."

Swampy: "Country very dry?"

Boss: "Yes. Looks like it."

Swampy: "A fire 'ud be very bad just now?"

Boss: "Eh?"

Swampy: "Yes. Now I'm allers very careful with matches an' fire when I'm on the track."

Boss: "Are yer?"

Swampy: "Yes. I never lights a fire near the grass – allers in the middle of the track – it's the safest place yer can get. An' I allers put the fire out afore I leaves the camp. If there ain't no water ter spare I cover the ashes with dirt. An' some fellers are so careless with matches lightin' their pipes." *(Reflective pause.)*

Boss: "Are they?"

Swampy: "Yes. Now, when I lights me pipe on the track in dry weather I allers rubs the match head up an' drops it in the dust. I never drops a burnin' match. But some travellers is so careless. A chap might light his pipe an' fling the match away without thinkin' an' the match might fall in a dry tuft, an' – there yer are!" *(with a wave of his arms)*. "Hundreds of miles o' grass gone an' thousands o' sheep starvin'. Some fellers is so careless – they never thinks... An' what's more, they don't care if they burn the whole country."

Boss *(scratching his head reflectively)*: "Ah – umph! – You can go up to the store and get a bit of tucker. The storekeeper might let yer have a bit o' tobacco."

On one occasion when they were out of flour and meat, Brummy and Swampy came across two other pilgrims camped on a creek, who were also out of flour and meat. One of them had tried a surveyors' camp a little further down, but without success. The surveyors' cook had said that he was short of flour and meat himself. Brummy tried him – no luck. Then Swampy said *he'd* go and have a try. As luck would have it, the surveyors' cook was just going to bake; he had got the flour out in the dish, put in the salt and baking powder, mixed it up, and had gone to the creek for a billy of water when Swampy arrived.While the cook was gone Swampy slipped the flour out of the dish into his bag, wiped the dish, set it down again, and planted the bag behind a tree at a little distance. Then he stood waiting, holding a spare empty bag in his hand. When the cook came back he glanced at the dish, lowered the billy of water slowly to the ground, scratched his head, and looked at the dish again in a puzzled way.

"Blanked if I didn't think I got that flour out!" he said.

"What's that, mate?" asked Swampy.

"Why! I could have sworn I got the flour out in the dish and mixed it before I went for the water," said the cook, staring at the dish again. "It's rum what tricks your memory plays on you sometimes."

"Yes," said Swampy, showing interest, while the cook got some more flour out into the dish from a bag in the back of the tent. "It is strange. I've done the same thing meself. I suppose it's the heat that makes us all a bit off at times."

"Do you cook, then?" asked the surveyors' cook.

"Well, yes. I've done a bit of it in me time; but it's about played out. I'm after stragglers now." (Stragglers are stray sheep missed in the general muster and found about the out paddocks and shorn after the general shearing.)

They had a yarn and Swampy "bit the cook's ear" for a "bit o' meat an' tea an' sugar," not forgetting "a handful of flour if yer can spare it."

"Sorry," said the cook, "but I can only let you have about a pint. We're very short ourselves."

"Oh, that's all right!" said Swampy, as he put the stuff into his spare bags. "Thank you! Good-day!"

"Good-day," said the cook.

The cook went on with his work and Swampy departed, catching up the bag of flour from behind the tree as he passed it, and keeping the clump of timber well between him and the surveyors' camp, lest the cook should glance round, and, noticing the increased bulk of his load, get some new ideas concerning mental aberration.

Nearly every Bushman has at least one superstition, or notion, that lasts his time – as nearly every Bushman has at least one dictionary word which lasts him all his life. Brummy had a gloomy notion – Lord knows how he got it! – that he should'a' gone on the boards if his people hadn't been so ignorant. He reckoned

that he had the face and cut of an actor, could mimic any man's voice, and had wonderful control over his features. They came to a notoriously "hungry" station, where there was a Scottish manager and storekeeper. Brummy went up to "government house" in his own proper person, had a talk with the storekeeper, spoke of a sick mate, and got some flour and meat. They camped down the creek, and next morning Brummy started to shave himself.

"Whatever are you a-doin' of, Brummy?" gasped Swampy in great astonishment.

"Wait and see," growled Brummy, with awful impressiveness, as if he were going to cut Swampy's throat after he'd finished shaving. He shaved off his beard and whiskers, put on a hat and coat belonging to Swampy, changed his voice, dropped his shoulders, and went limping up to the station on a game leg. He saw the cook and got some "brownie," a bit of cooked meat and a packet of baking powder. Then he saw the storekeeper and approached the tobacco question. Sandy looked at him and listened with some slight show of interest, then he said:–

"Oh that's all right now! but you needn't ha' troublt shavin' yer beard – the cold weather's comin' on! An' yer mate's duds don't suit ye – they're too sma'; an' yer game leg doesn't fit ye either – it takes a lot o' practice. Ha' ye got ony tea an' sugar?"

Brummy must have touched something responsive in that old Scot somewhere, but *his* lack of emotion upset Brummy somewhat, or else an old deep-rooted superstition had been severely shaken. Anyway he let Swampy do the cadging for several days thereafter.

But one bad season they were very hard up indeed – even for Brummy and Swampy. They'd tramped a long hungry track, and had only met a few wretched jackeroos, driven out of the cities by hard times, and tramping hopelessly west. They were out of tobacco, and their trousers were so hopelessly "gone" behind that when they went to cadge at a place where there was a woman they were moved to back and sidle and edge away again – and neither Brummy nor Swampy was over-fastidious in matters of dress or personal appearance. It was absolutely necessary to earn a pound or two, so they decided to go to work for a couple of weeks. It wouldn't hurt them, and then there was the novelty of it.

They struck West-o'-Sunday Station, and the boss happened to want a rouseabout to pick up wool and sweep the floor for the shearers.

"I can put *one* of you on," he said. "Fix it up between yourselves and go to work in the morning."

Brummy and Swampy went apart to talk it over.

"Look here! Brum, old man," said Swampy, with great heartiness, "we've been mates for a long while now, an' shared an' shared alike. You've allers acted straight to me an' I want to do the fair thing by you. *I* don't want to stand in *your* light. You take the job an' I'll be satisfied with a pair of pants out of it and a bit o'tobacco now an' agen. There yer are! I can't say no fairer than that."

"Yes," said Brummy, resentfully, "an' you'll always be throwin' it up to me afterwards that I done you out of a job!"

"I'll swear I won't," said Swampy, hurriedly. "But since you're so blasted touchy and suspicious about it, *you* take this job an' I'll take the next that turns up. How'll that suit you?"

Brummy thought resentfully.

"Look here!" he said presently, "let's settle it and have done with this damned sentimental tommy-rot. I'll tell you what I'll do – I'll give you the job and take my chance. The boss might want another man to-morrow. Now, are you satisfied?"

But Swampy didn't look grateful or happy.

"Well," growled Brummy, "of all the – – – I ever travelled with you're the – – –. What do you want anyway? What'll satisfy you? That's all I want to know. Hey? – can't yer speak?"

"Let's toss up for it," said Swampy, sulkily.

"All right," said Brummy, with a big oath, and he felt in his pocket for two old pennies he had. But Swampy had got a suspicion somehow that one of those pennies had two heads on it, and he wasn't sure that the other hadn't two tails – also, he suspected Brummy of some skill in "palming," so he picked up a chip from the wood-heap, spat on it, and spun it into the air. "Sing out!" he cried, "wet or dry?"

"Dry," said Brummy, promptly. He had a theory that the wet side of the chip, being presumably heaviest, was more likely to fall downwards; but this time it was "wet" up three times in succession. Brummy ignored Swampy's hand thrown out in hearty congratulation; and next morning he went to work in the shed. Swampy camped down the river, and Brummy supplied him with a cheap pair of moleskin trousers, tucker and tobacco. The shed cut out within three weeks and the two sundowners took the track again, Brummy with two pounds odd in his pocket – he having negotiated his cheque at the shed.

But now there was suspicion, envy and distrust in the hearts of those two wayfarers. Brummy was now a bloated capitalist, and proud, and anxious to get rid of Swampy – at least Swampy thought so. He thought that the least that Brummy might have done was to have shared the "stuff" with him.

"Look here, Brummy," he said reproachfully, "we've shared and shared alike, and – –"

"We never shared money," said Brummy, decidedly.

"Do you think I want yer blasted money?" retorted Swampy indignantly. "When did I ever ask yer for a sprat? Tell me that!"

"You wouldn't have got it if you had asked," said Brummy, uncompromisingly. "Look here!" with vehemence. "Didn't I keep yer in tobacco and buy yer gory pants? What are you naggin' about anyway?"

"Well," said Swampy, "all I was goin' to say was that yer might let me carry one of them quids in case you lost one – yer know you're careless and lose things; or in case anything happened to you."

"I ain't going to lose it – if that's all that's fretting you," said Brummy, "and there ain't nothing going to happen to me – and don't you forget it."

"That's all the thanks I get for givin' yer my gory job," said Swampy, savagely. "I won't be sich a soft fool agen, I can tell yer."

Brummy was silent, and Swampy dropped behind. He brooded darkly, and it's a bad thing for a man to brood in the Bush. He was reg'lar disgusted with Brummy. He'd allers acted straight to him, and Brummy had acted like a "cow." He'd stand it no longer; but he'd have some satisfaction. He wouldn't be a fool. If Brummy was mean skunk enough to act to a mate like that, Swampy would be even with him; he would wait till Brummy was asleep, collar the stuff, and clear. It was his job, anyway, and the money was his by rights. He'd have his rights.

Brummy, who carried the billy, gave Swampy a long tramp before he camped and made a fire. They had tea in silence, and smoked moodily apart until Brummy turned in. They usually slept on the ground, with a few leaves under them, or on the sand where there was any, each wrapped in his own blankets, and with their spare clothes, or rags rather, for pillows. Presently Swampy turned in and pretended to sleep, but he lay awake watching, and listened to Brummy's breathing. When he thought it was safe he moved cautiously and slipped his hand under Brummy's head, but Brummy's old pocket-book – in which he carried some dirty old letters in a woman's handwriting – was not there. All next day Swampy watched Brummy sharply every time he put his hands into his pockets, to try and find out in which pocket he kept his money. Brummy seemed very cheerful and sociable, even considerate, to his mate all day, and Swampy pretended to be happy. They yarned more than they had done for many a day. Brummy was a heavy sleeper, and that night Swampy went over him carefully and felt all his pockets, but without success. Next day Brummy seemed in high spirits – they were nearing Bourke, where they intended to loaf round the pubs for a week or two. On the third night Swampy waited till about midnight, and then searched Brummy, every inch of him he could get at, and tickled him with a straw of grass till he turned over, and ran his hands over the other side of him, and over his feet (Brummy slept with his socks on), and looked in his boots, and in the billy and in the tucker-bags, and felt in every tuft of grass round the camp, and under every bush, and down a hollow stump, and up a hollow log: but there was no pocket-book. Brummy couldn't have lost the money and kept it dark – he'd have gone back to look for it at once. Perhaps he'd thrown away the book and sewn the money in his clothes somewhere. Swampy crept back to him and felt the lining of his hat, and was running his hand over Brummy's chest when Brummy suddenly started to snore, and Swampy desisted without loss of time. He crept back to bed, breathing short, and thought hard. It struck him that there was something aggressive about that snore. He began to suspect that Brummy was up to his little game, and it pained him.

Next morning Brummy was decidedly frivolous. At any other time Swampy would have put it down to a "touch o' the sun," but now he felt a growing conviction that Brummy knew what he'd been up to the last three nights, and the more he thought of it the more it pained him – till at last he could stand it no longer.

"Look here, Brummy," he said frankly, "where the hell do you keep that flamin' stuff o'yourn? I been tryin' to get at it ever since we left West-o'-Sunday."

"I know you have, Swampy," said Brummy, affectionately – as if he considered that Swampy had done his best in the interests of mateship.

"I *knowed* yer knowed!" exclaimed Swampy, triumphantly. "But where the blazes did yer put it?"

"Under *your* head, Swampy, old man," said Brummy, cheerfully.

Swampy was hurt now. He commented in the language that used to be used by the bullock-punchers of the good days as they pranced up and down by their teams and lammed into the bullocks with saplings and crow-bars, and called on them to lift a heavy load out of a bog in the bed of a muddy creek.

"Never mind, Swampy!" said Brummy, soothingly, as his mate paused and tried to remember worse oaths. "It wasn't your fault."

But they parted at Bourke. Swampy had allers acted straight ter Brummy – share 'n' share alike. He'd do as much for a mate as any other man, an' put up with as much from a mate. He had put up with a lot from Brummy: he'd picked him up on the track and learned him all he knowed; Brummy would have starved many a time if it hadn't been for Swampy; Swampy had learned him how to "battle." He'd stick to Brummy yet, but he couldn't stand ingratitude. He hated low cunnin' an' suspicion, and when a gory mate got suspicious of his own old mate and wouldn't trust him, an' took to plantin' his crimson money – it was time to leave him.

Enter Mitchell

HE WESTERN TRAIN HAD JUST ARRIVED AT Redfern railway-station with a lot of ordinary passengers and one swagman.

He was short, and stout, and bow-legged, and freckled, and sandy. He had red hair and small, twinkling, grey eyes, and – what often goes with such things – the expression of a born comedian. He was dressed in a ragged, well-washed print shirt, an old black waistcoat with a calico back, a pair of cloudy moleskins patched at the knees and held up by a plaited greenhide belt buckled loosely round his hips, a pair of well-worn, fuzzy blucher boots, and a soft felt hat, green with age, and with no brim worth mentioning, and no crown to speak of. He swung a swag on to the platform, shouldered it, pulled out a billy and water-bag, and then went to a dogbox in the brakevan.

Five minutes later he appeared on the edge of the cab-platform with an anxious-looking cattle-dog crouching against his legs, and one end of the chain in his hand. He eased down the swag against a post, turned his face to the city, tilted his hat forward, and scratched the well-developed back of his head with a little finger. He seemed undecided what track to take.

"Cab, sir!"

The swagman turned slowly and regarded cabby with a quiet grin.

"Now, do I look as if I want a cab?"

"Well, why not? No harm, anyway – I thought you might want a cab."

Swaggy scratched his head, reflectively.

"Well," he said, "you're the first man that has thought so these ten years. What do I want with a cab?"

"To go where you're going, of course."

"Do I look knocked up?"

"I didn't say you did."

"And I didn't say you said I did... Now, I've been on the track this five years. I've tramped two thousan' miles since last Chris'mas, and I don't see why I can't tramp the last mile. Do you think my old dog wants a cab?"

The dog shivered and whimpered; he seemed to want to get away from the crowd.

"But then, you see, you ain't going to carry that swag through the streets, are you?" asked the cabman.

"Why not? Who'll stop me? There ain't no law agin it, I b'lieve?"

"But then, you see, it don't look well, you know."

"Ah! I thought we'd get to it at last."

The traveller up-ended his bluey against his knee, gave it an affectionate pat, and then straightened himself up and looked fixedly at the cabman.

"Now, look here!" he said, sternly and impressively, "can you see anything wrong with that old swag o' mine?"

It was a stout, dumpy swag, with a red blanket on the outside, patched with blue, and the edge of a blue blanket showing in the inner rings at the end. The swag might have been newer; it might have been cleaner; it might have been hooped with decent straps, instead of bits of clothes-line and greenhide – but otherwise there was nothing the matter with it, as swags go.

"I've humped that old swag for years," continued the bushman; "I've carried that old swag thousands of miles – as that old dog knows – an' no one ever bothered about the look of it, or of me, or of my old dog, neither; and do you think I'm going to be ashamed of that old swag, for a cabby or anyone else? Do you think I'm going to study anybody's feelings? No one ever studied mine! I'm in two minds to summon you for using insulting language towards me!"

He lifted the swag by the twisted towel which served for a shoulder-strap, swung it into the cab, got in himself and hauled the dog after him.

"You can drive me somewhere where I can leave my swag and dog while I get some decent clothes to see a tailor in," he said to the cabman. "My old dog ain't used to cabs, you see."

Then he added, reflectively: "I drove a cab myself, once, for five years in Sydney."

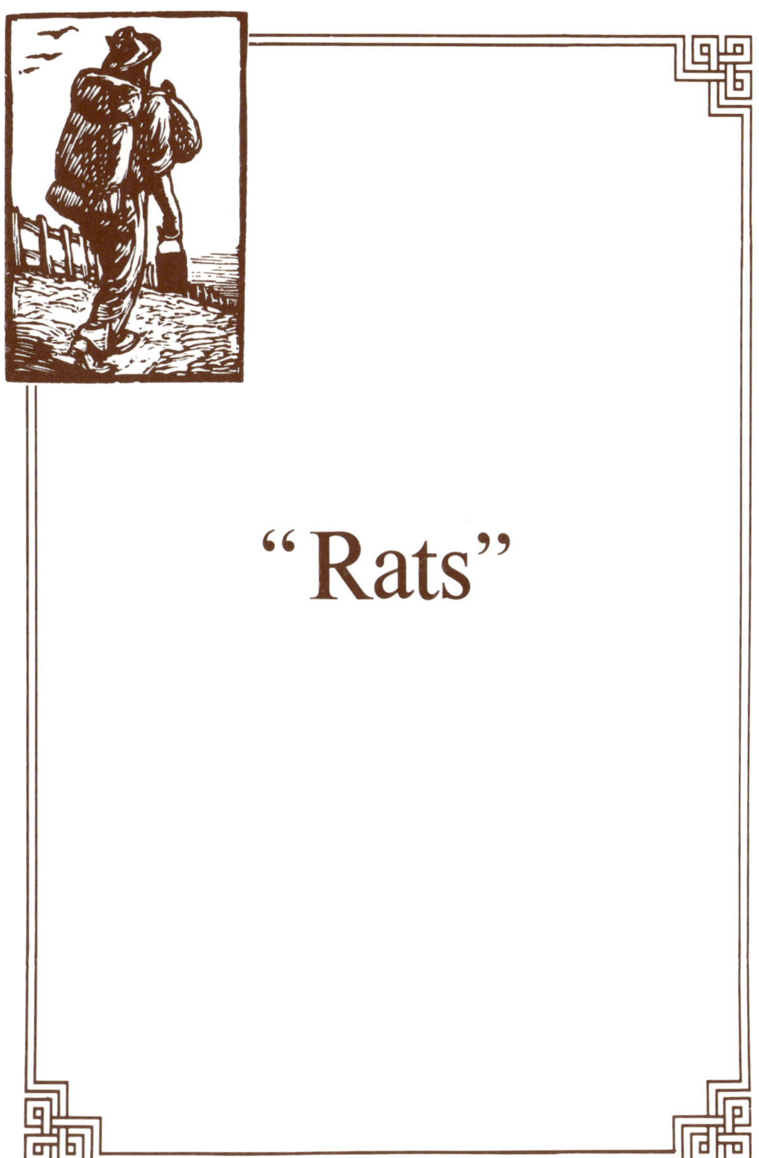

"Rats"

WHY, THERE'S TWO OF THEM, AND THEY'RE having a fight! Come on."

It seemed a strange place for a fight – that hot, lonely cotton-bush plain. And yet not more than half-a-mile ahead there were apparently two men struggling together on the track.

The three travellers postponed their smoke-ho and hurried on. They were shearers – a little man and a big man, known respectively as "Sunlight" and "Macquarie," and a tall, thin, young jackeroo whom they called "Milky."

"I wonder where the other man sprang from? I didn't see him before," said Sunlight.

"He muster bin layin' down in the bushes," said Macquarie. "They're goin' at it proper, too. Come on! Hurry up and see the fun!"

They hurried on.

"It's a funny-lookin' feller, the other feller," panted Milky.

"He don't seem to have no head. Look! he's down – they're both down! They must ha' clinched on the ground. No! they are up an' at it again… Why, good Lord! I think the other's a woman!"

"My oath! so it is!" yelled Sunlight. "Look! the brute's got her down again! He's kickin' her! Come on, chaps; come on, or he'll do for her!"

They dropped swags, water-bags and all, and raced forward; but presently Sunlight, who had the best eyes, slackened his pace and dropped behind. His mates glanced back at his face, saw a peculiar expression there, looked ahead again, and then dropped into a walk.

They reached the scene of the trouble, and there stood a little withered old man by the track, with his arms folded close up under his chin; he was dressed mostly in calico patches; and half-a-dozen corks, suspended on bits of string from the brim of his hat, dangled before his bleared optics to scare away the flies. He was scowling malignantly at a stout, dumpy swag which lay in the middle of the track.

"Well, old Rats, what's the trouble?" asked Sunlight.

"Oh, nothing, nothing," answered the old man, without looking round. "I fell out with my swag, that's all. He knocked me down, but I've settled him."

"But look here," said Sunlight, winking at his mates, "we saw you jump on him when he was down. That ain't fair, you know."

"But you didn't see it all," cried Rats, getting excited. "He hit *me* down first! And, look here, I'll fight him again for nothing, and you can see fair play."

They talked awhile; then Sunlight proposed to second the swag, while his mate supported the old man, and after some persuasion, Milky agreed, for the sake of the lark, to act as time-keeper and referee.

Rats entered into the spirit of the thing; he stripped to the waist, and while he was getting ready the travellers pretended to bet on the result.

Macquarie took his place behind the old man, and Sunlight up-ended the swag. Rats shaped and danced round; then he rushed, feinted, ducked, retreated, darted in once more, and suddenly went down like a shot on the broad of his back. No actor could have done it better; he went down from that imaginary blow as if a cannonball had struck him in the forehead.

Milky called time, and the old man came up, looking shaky. However, he got in a tremendous blow which knocked the swag into the bushes.

Several rounds followed with varying success.

The men pretended to get more and more excited, and betted freely; and Rats did his best. At last they got tired of the fun; Sunlight let the swag lie after Milky called time, and the jackeroo awarded the fight to Rats. They pretended to hand over the stakes, and then went back for their swags, while the old man put on his shirt.

Then he calmed down, carried his swag to the side of the track, sat down on it and talked rationally about bush matters for awhile; but presently he grew silent and began to feel his muscles and smile idiotically.

"Can you len' us a bit o' meat?" said he suddenly.

They spared him half-a-pound; but he said he didn't want it all, and cut off about an ounce, which he laid on the end of his swag.

Then he took the lid off his billy and produced a fishing-line. He baited the hook, threw the line across the track, and waited for a bite. Soon he got deeply interested in the line, jerked it once or twice, and drew it in rapidly. The bait had been rubbed off in the grass. The old man regarded the hook disgustedly.

"Look at that!" he cried, "I had him, only I was in such a hurry. I should ha' played him a little more."

Next time he was more careful, he drew the line in warily, grabbed an imaginary fish and laid it down on the grass. Sunlight and Co. were greatly interested by this time.

"Wot yer think o' that?" asked Rats. "It weighs thirty pound if it weighs an ounce! Wot yer think o' that for a cod? The hook's half-way down his blessed gullet!"

He caught several cod and a bream while they were there, and invited them to camp and have tea with him. But they wished to reach a certain shed next day, so – after the ancient had borrowed about a pound of meat for bait – they went on, and left him fishing contentedly.

But first Sunlight went down into his pocket and came up with half-a-crown, which he gave to the old man, along with some tucker. "You'd best push on to the water before dark, old chap," he said, kindly.

When they turned their heads again, Rats was still fishing: but when they looked back for the last time before entering the timber, he was having another row with his swag; and Sunlight reckoned that the trouble arose out of some lies which the swag had been telling about the bigger fish it caught.

LIONEL LINDSAY

Poems

ON THE WALLABY

Now the tent poles are rotting, the camp fires are dead,
And the possums may gambol in trees overhead;
I am humping my bluey far out on the land,
And the prints of my bluchers sink deep in the sand:
I am out on the wallaby humping my drum,
And I came by the tracks where the sundowners come.

It is nor'-west and west o'er the ranges and far
To the plains where the cattle and sheep stations are,
With the sky for my roof and the grass for my bunk,
And a calico bag for my damper and junk;
And scarcely a comrade my memory reveals,
Save the spiritless dingo in tow of my heels.

But I think of the honest old light of my home
When the stars hang in clusters like lamps from the dome,
And I think of the hearth where the dark shadows fall,
When my camp fire is built on the widest of all;
But I'm following Fate, for I know she knows best,
I follow, she leads, and it's nor'-west by west.

When my tent is all torn and my blankets are damp,
And the rising flood waters flow fast by the camp,
When the cold water rises in jets from the floor,
I lie in my bunk and I list to the roar,
And I think how to-morrow my footsteps will lag
When I tramp 'neath the weight of a rain-sodden swag.

Though the way of the swagman is mostly up-hill,
There are joys to be found on the wallaby still.
When the day has gone by with its tramp or its toil,
And your camp fire you light, and your billy you boil,
There is comfort and peace in the bowl of your clay
Or the yarn of a mate who is tramping that way.

But beware of the town – there is poison for years
In the pleasure you find in the depths of long beers;
For the bushman gets bushed in the streets of a town,
Where he loses his friends when his cheque is knocked
  down;
He is right till his pockets are empty, and then –
He can hump his old bluey up country again.

[Brisbane, July 1891 (revised August 1891)]

I'LL TELL YOU WHAT, YOU WANDERERS

I tell you what, you wanderers, who drift from town to town;
Don't look into a good girl's eyes, until you've settled down.
It's hard to go away alone and leave old chums behind –
It's hard to travel steerage when your tastes are more refined –
To reach a place when times are bad, and to be stranded there,
No money in your pocket nor a decent rag to wear.
But to be forced from that fond clasp, from that last clinging kiss –
By poverty! There is on earth no harder thing than this.

[December 1894]

TO A PAIR OF BLUCHER BOOTS

Old acquaintance unforgotten,
  Though you may be "ugly brutes" –
Though your leather's cracked and rotten,
  Worn-out pair of Blucher boots.

'Tis the richer man before you,
  Dearer leathers grace his feet;
'Twas the better man that wore you
  In the tramps through dust and heat!

Oft rebuffed by "super's" snarling,
  When I asked him for a "show",
On that long tramp to the Darling
  In the days of long ago;

Tell me, if you know it, whether,
  As I sadly tramped away,
Bore I heavy on your leather,
  Worn-out pair of Bluchers, say?

Though your leather's cracked and rotten,
  Though you may be ugly brutes,
I'll preserve you unforgotten,
  Worn-out pair of Blucher boots!

[April 1890]

THE SWAGMAN AND HIS MATE

From north to south throughout the year
  The shearing seasons run,
The Queensland stations start to shear
  When Maoriland has done;
But labour's cheap and runs are wide,
  And some the track must tread
From New Year's Day till Christmastide
  And never get a shed!
North, west, and south – south, west and north –
  They lead and follow Fate –
The stoutest hearts that venture forth –
  The swagman and his mate.

A restless, homeless class they are
  Who tramp in Borderland.
They take their rest 'neath moon and star –
  Their bed the desert sand,
On sunset tracks they ride and tramp,
  Till speech has almost died,
And still they drift from camp to camp
  In silence side by side.
They think and dream, as all men do;
  Perchance their dreams are great –
Each other's thoughts are sacred to
  The swagman and his mate.

With scrubs beneath the stifling skies
  Unstirred by heaven's breath;
Beyond the Darling Timber lies
  The land of living death!

A land that wrong-born poets brave
   Till dulled minds cease to grope –
A land where all things perish, save
   The memories of Hope.
When daylight's fingers point out back
   (And seem to hesitate)
The far faint dust cloud marks their track –
   The swagman and his mate.

And one who followed through the scrub
   And out across the plain,
And only in a bitter mood
   Would seek those tracks again,
Can only write what he has seen –
   Can only give his hand –
And greet those mates in words that mean
   "I know", "I understand."

I hope they'll find the squatter "white",
   The cook and shearers "straight",
When they have reached the shed to-night –
   The swagman and his mate.

[1896]

THE PAROO

It was a week from Christmas-time,
  As near as I remember,
And half a year since in the rear
  We'd left the Darling Timber.
The track was hot and more than drear;
  The long day seemed forever;
But now we knew that we were near
  Our camp – the Paroo River.

With blighted eyes and blistered feet,
  With stomachs out of order,
Half mad with flies and dust and heat
  We'd crossed the Queensland Border.
I longed to hear a stream go by
  And see the circles quiver;
I longed to lay me down and die
  That night on Paroo River.

'Tis said the land out West is grand –
  I do not care who says it –
It isn't even decent scrub,
  Nor yet an honest desert;
It's plagued with flies, and broiling hot,
  A curse is on it ever;
I really think that God forgot
  The country round that river.

My mate – a native of the land –
  In fiery speech and vulgar,
Condemned the flies and cursed the sand,
  And doubly damned the mulga.
He peered ahead, he peered about –
  A bushman he, and clever –
"Now mind you keep a sharp look-out;
  We must be near the river."

The "nose-bags" heavy on each chest
   (God bless one kindly squatter!)
With grateful weight our hearts they pressed –
   We only wanted water.
The sun was setting (in the west)
   In colour like a liver –
We'd fondly hoped to camp and rest
   That night on Paroo River.

A cloud was on my mate's broad brow,
   And once I heard him mutter:
"I'd like to see the Darling now,
   God bless the Grand Old Gutter!"
And now and then he stopped and said
   In tones that made me shiver –
"It cannot well be on ahead,
   I *think we've crossed the river.*"

But soon we saw a strip of ground
   That crossed the track we followed –
No barer than the surface round,
   But just a little hollowed.
His brows assumed a thoughtful frown –
   This speech he did deliver:
"I wonder if we'd best go down
   Or up the blessed river?"

"But where," said I, " 's the blooming stream?"
   And he replied, "We're at it!"
I stood awhile, as in a dream,
   "Great Scott!" I cried, "is *that* it?
Why, that is some old bridle-track!"
   He chuckled, "Well, I never!
It's nearly time you came out-back –
   This *is* the Paroo River!"

No place to camp – no spot of damp –
  No moisture to be seen there;
If e'er there was, it left no sign
  That it had ever been there.
But ere the morn, with heart and soul
  We'd cause to thank the Giver –
We found a muddy water-hole
  Some ten miles down the river.

[1893]

THE PROFESSIONAL WANDERER

When you've knocked about the country – been away from home
  for years;
When the past, by distance softened, nearly fills your eyes with
  tears –
You are haunted oft, wherever or however, you may roam,
By a fancy that you ought to go and see the folks at home.
You forget the family quarrels – little things that used to jar –
And you think of how they'll worry – how they wonder where
  you are;
You will think you served them badly, and your own part you'll
  condemn,
And it strikes you that you'll surely be a novelty to them,
For your voice has somewhat altered, and your face has somewhat
  changed –
And your views of men and matters over wider fields have ranged.
Then it's time to save your money, or to watch it (how it goes!);
Then it's time to get a "Gladstone" and a decent suit of clothes,
Then it's time to practise daily with a hair-brush and a comb,
Till you drop in unexpected on the folks and friends at home.

When you've been at home for some time, and the novelty's
  worn off,
And old chums no longer court you, and your friends begin to
  scoff;
When "the girls" no longer kiss you, crying "Jack! how you
  have changed!"
When you're stale to your relations, and their manner seems
  estranged;

When the old domestic quarrels, round the table thrice a day,
Make it too much like the old times – make you wish you'd stayed
away,
When, in short, you've spent your money in the fulness of your
heart,
And your clothes are getting shabby… Then it's high time
to depart.

[1897?]